Werewolf

Werewolf

COLIN DUNNE

This book is for the *real*
Lydia Wicks

Published in Great Britain in 1999
by Madcap Books,
André Deutsch Ltd, 76 Dean Street, London W1V 5HA

The right of Colin Dunne to be identified as the author of this work
has been asserted by him in accordance with the Copyright,
Designs and Patents Act, 1988

A catalogue record for this book is available from the British
Library

ISBN 0 233 99580 3

Printed in Great Britain

Chapter 1

It was the worst day of my life. I'm talking about the day when Maxie went crazy. At least, we thought she'd gone crazy.

First I'd better tell you all about myself. Name: Lyddie (Lydia when I'm in trouble). Age: thirteen in November (okay, twelve). Born in Boston, USA, last three years lived in England.

More tall than short, more thin than fat, good at tennis, unpopular at school, and kinda mixed up at the minute.

I'll tell you why. Dad was a real successful guy with a big marketing company in London. Big house out in Kent, beams, ingle-nook fireplaces, ponies in the paddock, three labradors and one dachshund, and me boarding at an expensive private school.

Then, one day, Dad's business goes down the tube because his partner's cheated him. Goodbye house, school, ponies, paddock and the lot. Mom and Dad move into a small flat in London to try to sort things out, and I'm shipped off to my Auntie Pauline in Ackerford, a sort of run-down old mining town north of Newcastle, and all I've got left from my old life is Maxie the Daxie (a she, actually, but I couldn't resist the name).

She was lovely, the only thing I had left from my previous life – I used to smuggle her up to my bed when Auntie Pauline wasn't looking – but very timid. When strangers came near she used to kinda huddle up to my legs, and she was so scared of other dogs that I had to pick her up every time one passed.

So it wasn't all that surprising that night when she wouldn't go out. I was scared of her making a mess in the house, because Auntie Pauline didn't like pets anyway. This night she cowered back under the kitchen table and whimpered.

'Put her out, Lydia,' said my auntie, in her ratty voice – she always called me Lydia. 'I don't want to come down to a mess on the floor.'

'Yes, Auntie,' I said, and reached under the table to get hold of Maxie's collar. I had to drag her, nails scraping on the tiles, all the way to the back door and when I opened it she wriggled like mad, trying to escape. But I more or less threw her out and slammed the door.

Auntie Pauline gave me an irritated blink. 'She's no trouble,' I said, really feebly. Mom and Dad had told me how kind it was of Auntie Pauline to take me in while they tried to sort out our lives – and I knew it was, so I always tried to be helpful, I really did try.

'No trouble to you perhaps, Lydia,' Auntie Pauline said. 'But if I wished to have a dog I would have one of my own.'

She bent down and wiped an imaginary mark off the kitchen floor. She was very house-proud. Mom wasn't. Our old house was untidy, but it sure was homey.

'There's something else I've been meaning to speak to you about, Lydia,' she went on. She was the only one who called me Lydia in full: to everyone else I was Lyddie.

'Oh yes,' I said, dreading what was coming next.

'You're a well-spoken young woman – I suppose at twelve I mustn't call you a girl any more – despite your American accent, but I have noticed you're picking up the local accent.'

That was why I was unpopular at school – because of the way I spoke. An American who'd been to private school in the South – Posh Yank they called me. Trying to speak the way the others did was my only chance of survival.

'After all the money your parents spent on your education, I don't think they would care to hear that. And do take your school books up to your room.'

'Yes, Auntie,' I said, and picked them up off the brightly polished kitchen table.

And up I went to My Room. It didn't feel like mine. It was too tidy for a start. I stared out of the window over the fields at the back which led up to the Northumberland hills. In the dark, I could only see the patch of the garden at the back which was lit by the kitchen light.

I wasn't happy there, but I never told anyone. It really was kind of Auntie Pauline to give me a home.

Mom and Dad said I'd have to be patient, so I was. They'd gotten enough worries without me being tricky. So I tried to fit in with everyone at school here in the North, although I don't think they wanted to fit in with me. Two months I'd been there. But I knew – and Mom and Dad always told me – that it wouldn't last for ever, and soon we'd all be together again. I could stand anything as long as I knew that was true.

Then I heard Maxie yelping outside. Only it was more than a yelp, a sort of high-pitched scream, and I could hear her flinging herself against the door. Something must be attacking her.

I rushed downstairs. Auntie Pauline was staring at the door. 'That creature is tearing the paint off the door,' she said, looking horrified. 'This really is too much.'

If only I'd known how right she was I would never have opened that door. A minute later, I wished I hadn't.

Chapter 2

The door was only open an inch or two when Maxie came flying through like a tornado.

The next few minutes were total mayhem. Jeez, she flew around the kitchen like a tiny brown bomb. Hurtling and skidding over the tiles, she sent everything flying, then she was up on the chairs and table. The table lamp and a glass vase crashed to the ground and smashed into splinters. All the time she was yelping and growling.

Auntie Pauline had backed up to the door with her hands in front of her face in terror. I was terrified too, but I had to do something, so I tried to grab Maxie from the table and talk calmly to her.

'Come on, sweetie-pie Maxie,' I said (that's how I talked to her!) 'Don't be a silly pup.'

She flew for my throat. For that second, she seemed much bigger, her teeth like long fangs, but that was probably just in the terror of the moment. Anyway, I flung up my arms too – a reflex, I guess – and she twisted in mid-air, landing on the window-sill. There was the crash of more ornaments hitting the deck.

'Quick!' yelled Auntie Pauline. She'd half-opened the door into the hall and I followed her through it as fast as I could. Outside, we both stood panting, staring at each other. What the hell was going on?

'I'll ring Mr Maultby,' I said. Chris Maultby was the vet. Plus he was also the local hottie. In his twenties, always wore jeans (real neat ass!) and very cool – not that I was thinking about that.

'And Andy Squires,' said my auntie. He was the local cop, a nice old guy.

I got Chris Maultby on his mobile and he said he'd come straight away, and PC Squires said the same. Me and my auntie just stood in the hall, listening to the row and the sounds of destruction inside, not knowing what to say, and it seemed ages before I saw headlamps outside.

I ran out. It was the vet. I told him what had happened and he nodded and got a bag out of his van. He put on some real heavy-duty gloves, like shipyard workers wear, and prepared a hypodermic needle and some other medical-type stuff.

'Let's have a look at her,' he said. He'd seen Maxie before when she'd cut herself on some barbed wire.

Outside the kitchen door, he listened for a few minutes, and PC Squires arrived then, huffing and puffing – he was a tubby guy. 'Sounds bad,' Chris said to the policeman, as he eased the door open a fraction.

'I'll come in with you,' said PC Squires.

'Not without protective clothing, you won't,' said Chris, and he slipped through the door and slammed it behind him.

The cop asked me a few questions about Maxie – all I could say was that she was a quiet little thing – but really we were all listening. At first the growling and barking got worse. We could hear the vet talking in a quiet, soothing voice. Then there was the sound of a bit of a struggle. Chris swore, then silence.

We all looked at each other. What was going on?

PC Squires had taken off his helmet and put it on the hall table. He rubbed his big red face with his hands and patted down his grey hair. I think he must have been dozing when we rang – although you'd think this was enough to wake anyone up.

'I'm going in,' he said, and cautiously opened the door. Nothing happened. He opened it wide and we saw Chris Maultby holding Maxie down on the table.

'Oh my God, look at the room!' wailed Auntie Pauline, and it was true, the dog had trashed the place.

We followed PC Squires in. Chris had pinned Maxie down on top of the table with one gloved hand around her neck. In his other he was holding the hypodermic needle. He was watching the dog carefully and you could see her back legs were still twitching.

'I've given her enough to drop a horse,' the vet said, waving the needle. 'Two lots. I think that's knocked her out.'

Taking the scene in – the wrecked kitchen and the flat-out dog – PC Squires edged nearer, pretty cautiously too. 'What the hell happened?' was all he could say.

'Well,' Chris shot a quick look at me and my auntie, obviously thinking about what he was going to say, 'I've never come across anything like this before.'

'Rabies!' Auntie Pauline shrieked, drawing back.

'Don't let's panic,' said PC Squires, patting her on the arm.

'Is Maxie all right?' I asked.

Chris Maultby gave my auntie a serious look. 'We don't want any talk of rabies at this point,' he said. 'We don't want any wild rumours in the town. Lyddie,' he said, turning me to me, 'Maxie isn't all right, not by any means.'

'You'll want to get her down to your clinic,' said the cop.

Chris Maultby studied the trapped dog. She looked tiny again now, quivering a little as she lay there, and I couldn't help but see the white spittle bubbling around her mouth. What if it was rabies? My poor little pup.

'Were you bitten?' PC Squires asked, as he suddenly thought of it. 'Either of you?' There was a real urgency in the way he asked.

Auntie Pauline looked at me. 'No,' she said. 'Thank God. Neither of us was bitten.'

'That's the most important thing,' said the vet. 'Come on, Andy, give me a hand to get the dog in here.'

My little pet was all floppy now. They gingerly slipped her into a big wire mesh cage and took her out to the van. It was a still night, with a bright moon overhead.

As Chris was slipping off his gauntlets, I asked him again if Maxie would be all right. 'I've got a lot of tests to do,' he said, as he closed the doors. 'I'll have to send some samples down to Newcastle and then we'll soon find out. It will only take a day or two.'

'She's not coming back here!' said Auntie Pauline.

'Don't let's rush things,' said the vet. Then he put his hand on my shoulder and spoke to me in a kindly voice. 'I'll look after her, don't worry. But I don't want you to visit her until I've got full reports. I'll give you a call.'

We watched the van and the policeman's little Fiesta go off down the empty street.

'I'm sorry, Auntie, I really am,' I said. 'Look, I'll do all the clearing up. You sit down, you've had a terrible shock.'

I was wondering if she'd throw me out as well as Maxie, but she surprised me. She took a deep breath and put her arms round me. 'We'll do it together, Lydia. I know how much you love that little dog and you've had so many nasty shocks lately.'

Kindness, when it's sort of unexpected, shakes you. I started to cry and she held me a little closer. Back we went inside, to the wrecked room, and just as I was closing the door, I heard a long, piercing howl from the hills at the back.

'A fox,' said Auntie Pauline. 'That's all we need.'

Some fox, I thought. The night air was cold on my tear-soaked face. But that wasn't why I was shivering.

Chapter 3

How do rumours like that spread? Next morning you'd think it had been on television – the school was buzzing with it.

For a change, I was a bit of a star. They all wanted to know what had happened and was it true that my dog had gone mad and bitten half the people in the street – the way some people exaggerate.

In the locker-room, when I was unloading some of the junk from my rucksack, Mickey Scudd was running round on all fours growling and pretending to be a mad dog. That was a bit upsetting when I thought about poor old Maxie, but it was better than the usual teasing.

Posh Yank – that's how they saw me. It didn't help when I had problems understanding the local Geordie accent, but I was beginning to get the hang of it now.

I wasn't angry about it. It was only because I was, well, different, and kids don't like people to be different.

And Ackerford was a bit cut-off. There were a couple of old Victorian buildings, like the library and the council offices, there were still rows of old terraces, but most of the families lived in the two big council estates on the edge of town. The school, out on the Newcastle road, was a sprawling collection of single-storey buildings put up about twenty years ago, I guess.

To be honest, there was lots of graffiti and litter, but it was a poor part of the country. What I did like about it were the hills all around: great big black desolate empty hills – I loved walking in them with Maxie.

In our tutor room, where we had to go register every morning, I met up with my 'mates' (that's what they called them round there), and a pretty odd threesome we made.

At the start of term, all the others in Year Eight – who'd grown up together – raced off to get the best lockers and left me with Stipo and Stodge. We had to be pals: no one else wanted us. We were the outcasts, all three of us. We got the lockers with busted locks and bent doors.

Stipo came from somewhere in Eastern Europe and sometimes they called him gyppo and – which was what amazed me – he didn't seem to mind. 'I am gypsy,' he said. 'I am proud to be gypsy.' He lived in a row of three broken-down old houses with about twenty other refugees.

The older ones looked strange – long dresses, headscarves, worn faces, and they didn't speak much English. Most of the other people in the town were scared of them.

They had huge fires on the spare land on which they seemed to cook, and there were heaps of broken down cars all around.

I liked Stipo. He was small and quick and he spoke a funny sort of mixed up English. He'd even got three rings in his eyebrow, but the local boys didn't seem to trust him.

Stodge was . . . well, a Stodge, I suppose, He'd got a gland problem which meant he'd blown up into a real fat boy which is why they were so tough on him.

So there we were – a gang of three outcasts nobody else wanted – trooping into the tutor room while Mrs Waterhouse, Year 8 tutor, took the register. First she had some sad news for us. A little girl – two years old – had gone missing from a village just outside the town. She asked us to look out for a toddler in a red beret.

Mickey and two of the other boys weren't even listening – they were doing their stupid growling and running round.

'What's all this about?' asked Mrs Waterhouse.

'It's Lyddie,' said Mickey. 'Her dog's gone mad. It's the Beast of Ackerford.' The Beast of Ackerford was a sort of local legend – a big cat that was supposed to have escaped and be living in the hills – but they all pretended they believed it.

They all started laughing and pushing each other. Mrs Waterhouse gave a big sigh and called them to order. 'We've been over this before, haven't we?' she said. 'In almost every part of Britain there is a story of wild animal living in the countryside. Can anyone name them?'

'The Beast of Bodmin,' said a girl called Michelle. 'It eats sheep and cows. It does!' she added as the others began to groan.

'Did they have any near you in the South, Lyddie?' Mrs Waterhouse asked me. Mrs Waterhouse was nice. She tried to make me feel part of the class.

'Yes, there's one down there called the Surrey puma,' I said.

'Yeah and she brought it up here wi' 'er,' said Mickey Scudd. Everyone laughed, natch.

'Aye, an' it eats babies,' one of Mickey's mates shouted, and they all began growling again.

On our way to the PSE class Stipo fixed me with his serious brown eyes and asked me if I'd been telling the truth. I stopped and looked down into his little dark face. I told him it was a bit worse than that.

'Running round? Biting?' He said the words quickly as though he knew what he was talking about.

I looked around and nodded. 'The vet says not to talk about it too much. He doesn't want everyone scared of rabies.'

I thought that was what Stipo suspected too. But he pulled back and his eyebrows shot up in surprise. 'Rabies?' Then he laughed, a little chuckle that wasn't funny somehow. 'Is nothing. Is just a sick dog. Have you heard howling at night?'

'What?' Stodge's eyes went huge and round. 'Do you mean there really is a Beast of Ackerford?'

Stipo put his arms around both of us and

pulled us together. 'There are worse things than Ackerford Beast,' he whispered.

I laughed. Beasts wandering the countryside and haunted howling – it was all kinda silly. At the same time I remembered the howls I'd heard coming from the hills last night. And I wondered how Stipo knew. He knew other things too. You could see it in his dark sad eyes.

Chapter 4

It was all so different from my boarding school, but at the same time it was all the same. There they didn't hate you because you were different: there were girls from all over the world, all colours, all languages. But there were still rivalries and spite and, I suppose, hatred too. There, they would have teased the Northumberland kids for the way they spoke: here they teased me – fair enough in a way.

And there they would show off not by being tough but by who had the most expensive clothes and whose father had the biggest car. But in the end – I'd already learned this – it was just the same. Some kids were nice, some were nasty, and most were somewhere in the middle.

The next day, Mrs Waterhouse came over with

a message for me. Chris Maultby wanted me to call in after school. It didn't sound too good.

Poor Maxie. I felt a tug at my bag. It was Stipo.

'I come with you,' he whispered. 'Maybe she's okay.'

'Me too,' said Stodge.

'You're used to real big tragedies, I guess?' I said to Stipo.

Serious as ever, he nodded. 'Oh yes,' he said, in the same dry, steady voice. 'Mother, father, whole family gone. I have seen things no one should see.'

Now this is what I don't get. Something like that, your family dead and everything, was much worse than me and Maxie. But somehow, because Stipo's tragedy was a long way away and months ago, it didn't make my sadness any less. I felt guilty about that.

Outside Mr Maultby's clinic, which was an old Army hut spruced up and painted white, we stopped. 'You don't have to come in,' I said.

'Better you're not alone,' Stipo replied, and held the door open for me and Stodge.

Chris Maultby was in reception wiping his hands on a towel, a white coat on over his jeans. His thin handsome face was smiling, but the smile soon vanished when he saw me.

'Come through,' he said. 'PC Squires is here too.'

The cop nodded to us as we went in, and the vet slid round behind his big desk and sat down.

'There's no kind way to tell you, Lyddie,' he said, in a quiet voice. 'Maxie was very, very sick, and I had to put her down.'

Tears swelled into my eyes and overflowed down my face and I saw Stodge had tears in his too.

'Honestly, it was the best thing for her. You saw how she was – she was a desperately sick animal in pain, and now she feels no pain. I would've done it if it was my own dog.'

When you're upset you say such idiotic things. 'Thank you,' I said. Stipo squeezed my elbow. 'Was it . . .' I couldn't bring myself to say the word now it came to it '. . . Was it rabies?'

He shook his head. 'No, the lab down in Newcastle don't believe it was. But it was some sort of . . . well, madness to use the popular term. What we have to do is to try to work out the cause and make sure there are no more cases.'

Then PC Squires sat me down and asked me dozens of questions. Where I'd bought Maxie, if she'd had any sickness, what she'd been eating

. . . all sorts of things. But he asked them in a kind way, and even gave me his great big hanky to mop up my tears. And then he surprised me.

'Chris was saying Maxie had been in a fight?'

I frowned. Maxie was too timid to get in fights – she'd run a mile if another dog so much as looked at her. I told him this and Chris Maultby stepped in. 'I'm sorry, Lyddie, but there were two quite clear bite marks on her neck. Big ones too.'

I felt Stipo's fingers tighten on my arm so much it hurt, as though it meant something to him.

And I wondered if that was why Maxie had been yelping in the garden. Had another dog got in and attacked her? Or that fox. Maybe that was it.

As we were leaving, the vet solemnly handed over to me a cardboard box. I knew what was in it. 'I thought you'd like to give her a decent burial,' he said.

Stipo carried the box as we walked back to my auntie's house, and he even dug the grave in the front garden. 'I know what sadness is,' was all he said.

Stodge made a little cross out of two old

lollipop sticks and wrote 'Maxie the Daxie' on it and stuck it on her grave, and we all stood there for a minute, feeling awkward.

When I looked up, I saw a black car had slid silently up the road and halted outside the gate. It was a huge old-fashioned thing, like you see at funerals. The driver had wound down the window and he called me over. I thought he was lost so I went across to help.

When he spoke I realized he was foreign, with a thick accent. 'Are you ze girl wiz ze sick dog?'

I nodded.

'Gut,' he said. 'Ve are from an animal rescue centre at Mawkworth Hall. Ve thought perhaps ve could help wiz treatment.'

It was only then that I saw there was a figure in the back of the car. Although he was leaning forward to listen, I couldn't see him clearly because the car had darkly tinted windows. But I did get an impression of a long narrow face beneath a Russian-style fur hat.

'She's dead,' I said, the tears starting up again. 'We've just buried her.' I pointed to the cross. 'There!'

The driver turned and spoke to the man in the back in a foreign language. Then he turned back to me and began to wind the window up. 'Ve are most sorry,' he said, and drove off.

As it moved away, I saw the long narrow face pressed up to the glass. He wasn't looking at me. He wasn't looking at Stodge who was standing just behind me. He was looking up the side of the house.

Then I realized that Stipo wasn't in the front garden. He'd retreated into the shadows and it was him the man was staring at.

Once the car had gone, he stepped out again into the light. His face was pinched and white, as though he'd had the most terrible shock.

'Oh no,' he murmured. 'No, no, no. Pray God it isn't true.'

'What?' I said, in a panic. 'Say what isn't true? Do you know that man?'

He nodded. 'He comes from my home country.'

'Well, shouldn't you be glad to see him?'

He put his fingers to his mouth and began to twist his lips. 'No one is glad to see him.'

'Who is he?'

'He ... he ... he ...' Stipo couldn't get the words out and I could see he was shaking. Finally he managed it. 'He is the Count Lupus.'

Chapter 5

I got them both inside and fetched some Coke from the fridge. Thank the Lord that my auntie was at the Women's Institute meeting – she wouldn't have liked a gypsy boy in the house.

And Stipo had gone really strange. He sat in the corner of the kitchen, white-faced and silent, but I could see the glass of Coke was trembling in his hands. Whenever I asked him who Count Lupus was (and what a stupid name that was!), he'd only shake his head and say: 'Evil! You don't know what evil is.'

Stodge just looked baffled. 'He can't do anything to us,' he said.

Stipo replied: 'He has seen me. He has seen all of us.'

While we were sitting there, Stipo being all mysterious, it came on the local radio that another kid had gone missing. Ilyich, they said the name was, two years old . . . and from the refugee camp where Stipo lived. They mentioned fears of the Beast of Ackerford, and also that the police were having trouble getting information out of the gypsies.

Stipo sucked in his cheeks and I could hear his breathing quicken. 'I know him. Nice little kid.'

'Why won't your people help the police?'

'They are afraid,' he said.

'What?' said Stodge. 'Afraid of PC Squires?'

'No,' Stipo replied. 'They are afraid of Count Lupus. One minute,' he said, and suddenly got up and rushed out of the door. When he came back a minute later he was holding the lollipop stick marker we'd put on the grave. 'Now we must all be afraid.'

Then he told us why. It was hard to believe – he said it would be – but hearing his steady, quiet voice and seeing those dark eyes in his pale face, we didn't question a word of it.

Although they were now a legend, he told us, for centuries werewolves enjoyed a reign of terror throughout the countries of Eastern Europe. They would snatch young children to eat. Adults were petrified of being bitten which would turn them into werewolves. In towns and villages they bolted their doors at night and shook with fear when they heard the howling in the hills. Every person they bit, and every dog, too, would turn into a werewolf: that was how they built up their power.

Only in the last century did they stop being seen as two world wars shook up the whole of Europe and the modern world of television and cars began to touch these half-forgotten countries. 'But they have been there all along,' he said, his eyes narrowing. 'Waiting for their moment.'

Their moment was now. All the fighting in Bosnia and the Balkans had caused a great backwash of displaced people scuttling over all the borders. Thousands upon thousands of refugees had been forced to leave their native lands. And with them had come Count Lupus.

Picking his words with care, he looked first at Stodge and then at me. 'They wish to recreate the Ancient Empire of the Werewolves here.'

'So who exactly is Count Lupus?' I asked, twisting my fingers nervously.

'He is the Emperor. He is as old as the mountains. He cannot be destroyed. Sometimes he rules, sometimes he skulks in the shadows, but he is always there. Now he is ready to rule again. That is why he is here.'

'But why here?' asked Stodge.

Stipo gave a small, secret smile. 'Because you are so modern in this country that you will not – you cannot – believe in werewolves. You would rather believe in the Beast of Ackerford and such nonsense. Then from here he can spread throughout the world and claim back his old empire.'

It all fitted, like a crazy jigsaw. Too many strange things happening. Maxie going mad like that, first one, now two, children missing. But what could we do about it? I said that to him, and in reply he lifted his hand from inside his jacket and held up . . .

The lollipop cross. I could see Stodge's writing: "Maxie the Daxie".

'Why've you brought that in?' Stodge asked. 'I thought I'd made a right grand job of it.'

I sensed there was more to it, and I was right.

Stipo's bottom lip trembled as he spoke. 'It's all there is left.'

I had to ask him what on earth he meant before he went on. 'Maxie's gone!'

We all rushed outside. I grabbed a torch from the hallstand because it had got dark now. Its narrow yellow beam passed over the front garden. All that was left was a hole! Someone had dug up Maxie in her sad little coffin and taken her away! It seemed so pointless, so cruel, that I began to sob again, and Stodge held my hand, not knowing what to say. The whole world had gone mad,

'Who'd want to dig up my dead pet?' I managed to say.

'Count Lupus,' Stipo replied. 'He had bitten her. Maxie was turning into a werewolf. Count Lupus had come to claim one of his own.'

And from the humped black outline of the hills came a howl. It hung over the dark silhouette of the hills and ran through the quiet streets of the town. A howl of triumph.

Chapter 6

It was like a council of war. All three of us sat around the kitchen table and made plans.

The gypsy refugees knew all this, but were too scared to do anything. No one else, PC Squires for instance, would believe three schoolkids – they'd just laugh at us. So I said I reckoned it was up to us – the three outcasts. 'We can't stay here anyway – he's seen us and he knows that Stipo recognized him. We'll track him down, we'll prove that he's a were-wolf and show everyone what he's up to.'

'But . . .' Stodge's voice was wavering a little, 'Stipo says he can't be destroyed and . . .' His voice gave out.

Stipo put a hand on his shoulder. 'There are things – old gypsy tricks – we can use to protect ourselves. I show you.'

'Anyway,' I said, feeling really determined, 'we've got to destroy him before he destroys us. We don't want werewolves running wild in our country. And I want my little Maxie back in her grave.'

Stodge gave a small cheer and even Stipo gave a quick grin. We'd show them all: we'd take on the Empire of the Werewolves ourselves.

Right there and then, we decided to set off for Mawkworth Hall. I rang my mom and asked her if she'd tell Auntie Pauline I'd had to go on a field trip with the school. Stodge said he'd tell his parents that too, and Stipo just shrugged: with no family, no one would care where he was.

The other two went off to their homes to get whatever they'd need. I changed into a warm sweater, strong shoes, and a waterproof and packed my rucksack with food, a thermos of coffee, a torch, my sleeping bag – everything I could think of. We didn't know how long we'd be away.

In a funny way, it was quite exciting when I hoisted my rucksack on to my back and set off. It was dark now. When I got to St Hubert's church – our meeting point – Stipo was already there. I noticed he'd got his things –

and there weren't many of them – in one of those giveaway plastic bags. They really must be very poor, those gypsies. When Stodge came, he'd got scarves and gloves and goodness knows what – boy, was he well-prepared.

Stipo looked up at the sign outside the church. 'I didn't know it was called St Hubert's.' An eerie little smile touched his face. 'A good sign, I think.'

I didn't ask why. Stipo was full of little mysteries like that – and he wouldn't tell you if you asked, anyway.

So off we all set. As if by agreement, Stipo led the way, with me and Stodge tagging along behind. In Castle Street, I stopped at the bank and got some money out of the hole-in-the-wall (I'd still got all my birthday money in there and I could spend it how I wanted). We carried on over the canal bridge, past the level crossing and the shut-down station, past the Hadrian council estate where lights shone in every window, and then we were out in the country.

It was a narrow road, one I'd often walked with Maxie, with high banks and hedges on either side. With a bright moon overhead, we didn't need the torch, and we all sang as we marched. Although I couldn't help wondering what had happened to Maxie, and worrying about the fear I'd seen on Stipo's face, it was like setting out on a real adventure.

We walked and walked. Stodge was panting a bit up the hills, but I was fine – I'm pretty fit really. Stipo was amazing. When me and Stodge stopped to read the signposts and work out which way we should be going, he would lift his eyes to the stars and say: 'North,' and off he'd go, with us behind him. He seemed to have a natural feel for the countryside, as though he knew where he was.

It got colder and darker when the moon slid behind a cloud and I could feel the fear building up in me. What could we do – the three outcasts? And what did Stipo know about the Count? How could I hope to find my poor pet again? All the fears of the night began to come to me.

'Here at last!' said Stodge. He'd stopped. He shone the torch on a sign which read Mawkworth. I looked at my watch. Ten past eleven: we'd been walking for nearly three hours.

'Yeah, but where are we going to sleep?' I said. We all looked at each other, then Stodge spoke up. 'I've got an idea. Let's go down into the village – I've been here with my mum and dad.'

We followed Stodge this time. The village was just winding down for the night. In the village square, ringed with old stone cottages and a few shops, lights shone in only a few windows, and the last few stragglers were leaving the Moorland Arms.

Stodge obviously knew what he was doing. He marched up to the newsagents and shone his torch on the display panel which was packed with cards for baby-sitters wanted and second-hand bikes for sale. He wrote down the number of a cottage to let, before going straight to the telephone kiosk. He was smiling to himself.

We listened outside. To our amazement, he put on a deep, grown-up voice. First we heard him apologize for ringing at this time of night and then he enquired about renting a holiday cottage for the next few days. He made a few more notes, thanked someone and came out.

'Found one,' he said, and led us out of the village and up a steep hill. On the way, he explained. There were lots of holiday cottages around here and at this time of year they would be sure to be empty. He'd enquired about one: it was empty, and it was half a mile outside the village . . . just right for us. Stodge looked really pleased with himself. I don't think he'd ever done anything so clever in his life.

Lilac Cottage was where he'd said. Standing alone in a field, it was in complete darkness and looked well locked-up. Stodge had found the place, and it was Stipo who got us in. He climbed up the drainpipe like a monkey, produced a slim knife from his belt and within a minute the upstairs window had popped open.

The front door creaked open and there he was, finger to lips. He needn't have worried. It was deserted. We only switched on one small lamp, giggling a bit with mixed feelings of relief at finding somewhere to sleep – and guilt at being burglars. It certainly was turning out to be an adventure.

Then we heard it. The howl. But this time it was much nearer, much louder and went on vibrating in the air for what seemed an age. We all stood, frozen to the spot. That was why we were here, and now it didn't seem such a funny adventure after all.

Chapter 7

'**Q**uick!' Stipo snapped, a second later. 'What time is it?' He didn't have a watch. I told him it was just past eleven-thirty – long past our bedtimes but I suppose we were so excited that we hadn't noticed.

He asked Stodge where Mawkworth Hall was – apparently, half a mile north of here, over the moor at the back of our cottage. It was where the howl had come from. The same howl I'd heard the night Maxie went crazy. The same howl I'd heard after the Count had come to my house.

'We've got to find the nearest crossroads to the Hall,' Stipo went on, talking urgently now. 'We must get there by midnight.'

I was puzzled. 'Why?'

'Because,' and he swallowed hard before

carrying on, 'that's where the werewolves have their sacrifices. Midnight, at a crossroads. Let's go.' We dumped our bags and followed him out of the back door.

It was colder now. The moon was dim behind the clouds. The great hump of the moor rose up before us as we clambered over the garden wall and set off upwards.

It was hard going. The moor got steeper and steeper and still the brow was a long way off. At first, the springy grass wasn't bad to walk on, but then we were into heather which tripped us at every step, and bracken which slashed our hands as we pushed our way through. But Stipo kept up a fast pace, turning every now and again to hurry us on.

For a while we found an old carters' track which meant we could make better speed, but then we were back into the heather again. Stipo seemed to find his way by a sort of sixth sense. He'd pause to look at the stars, run his eyes over the bulging black hills which stood all around us, and then signal us on. It was uncanny.

Bending, panting, legs pumping against the gradient, I was struggling, but Stipo skipped over the land. Every now and again we had to stop and wait for the gasping Stodge to catch up. I'd guess he'd never played much tennis!

And that was a funny thought . . . all my old pals asleep in the dormitory. Somehow, when it struck me, I thought I'd rather be here with my mates, fighting this ancient, monstrous evil. Nothing was going to stop us.

The hillside began to level out. Now it was more of a soft curve, and a minute later we were at the top, knee deep in heather. Ahead of us, against a pale slot in the sky, I could just make out rolling hills, stretching as far as I could see.

Below us, the moor dropped as suddenly as it had risen, a long steep bank leading to a black wood. Beyond that I thought I could see a road beside a silver thread of a stream, and beyond that . . .

Mawkworth Hall.

It had to be. Stodge had said it was the only house for miles. From what I could see from here, it was kinda like your Houses of Parliament, an old, fancy sort of building in dark stone, all knobbly bits and turrets and those old-timey narrow windows. There were lights in three of them.

Suddenly the perfect quiet of the still night was ripped apart by a howl. It seemed to split the sky. The hair on the back of my neck bristled, my spine froze, and I saw Stodge jump in his tracks. It pierced the night, a frightening sound, and much, much nearer than it had been before.

At that moment I felt a movement in the air, a soft silent brushing which skimmed my hair, a shadow which swooped across the land, and all three of us dived into the heather.

Stiff as a board, I lay there, my face buried in the rough vegetation, my nose in damp, peat-smelling soil. I was waiting for death to strike me.

Something touched me on the shoulder. Hardly daring to look, I turned my face. I saw Stipo's face looking at me. 'It's okay,' he whispered, pointing upwards. 'Look, an owl.'

And so it was, circling in the sky above.

A bit ashamed, we all struggled to our feet and began the descent. It was harder than the climb up the other side. Instead of pumping our legs, we had to brace them against the slope of the hill, and me and Stodge kept slipping and skidding on the grass and heather. Stipo glided over it, of course.

What made it worse was that on this side of the moor a keen steady wind was in our faces, and with it came an icy drizzle. I buttoned up my waterproof and fastened the hood around my face, but it was still pretty miserable.

'Wish I'd tried harder in gym,' I heard Stodge mutter as he slipped and skidded along painfully on his butt. I almost laughed.

Down and down we went, following Stipo's footsteps until – to my delight – the land flattened out. In front of us was the wood, with only a derelict fence around its rim. We paused to get our breath back.

'What time is it?' Stipo asked, in a hushed voice.

'Five to midnight,' I whispered back, after a look at the Swatch that Dad had got me for my last birthday (when he had some money, that was!).

'Hell! We're not going to make it. Let's try anyway.'

And off he went, diving through the fence and into the wood. Would we be in time to see the sacrifice? And what would they be sacrificing? I shivered at the thought.

In the wood it was completely black. What light there was in the night sky didn't reach down here. Without daring to cuss or swear, I blundered along, crashing my ankles against tree stumps, trying to duck the jagged branches.

It was a relief to see the trees thinning and ahead of us a narrow country road. On the other side of the road was a high wall, the sort you find around the big estates that once belonged to aristocrats.

As we cleared the trees, Stipo dropped to his knees and motioned us to do the same. He wasn't going to step out into the open until he'd had a good look around.

I realized then that his life in a country ravaged by war must have taught him how to protect himself in times of danger, and I was glad, oh so glad, that he was with me.

He crept up beside Stodge and I could hear him saying, if this was the north-south road, was there one running east-west? Stodge thought there was, just around the corner.

Skirting the edge of the wood, but staying in its shadows, we slipped on through the night, with the huge stone wall of the estate on the other side. We'd only gone a few hundred yards when we saw the gates – twenty-feet high, made of iron – which led into Mawkworth Hall. As we drew nearer, I saw the long gravel drive which led up to the house. It was a spooky looking place, like a black sandcastle with dozens of stone ornaments stuck all over it.

It was hideously ugly. Despite the light in three windows, it seemed to stink of death. I felt the fear rise up in me again and knew, just knew, I was in the presence of something vile.

But Stipo wasn't interested. He waved us on, then after a few more yards, suddenly pushed me down into the ditch with Stodge. He slid in beside me.

He pressed his lips to my ear and even then I could only just hear the words: 'The crossroads.'

And sure enough, as the moon drifted clear of the clouds, I could see where the two roads, each only wide enough for one car, intersected.

There was even a signpost.

The moon brightened again. I stared hard.

There, in the middle of the crossroads, some sort of creature stood. It was facing us, its nose raised into the sky.

Then I felt my heart lift and I jumped out of the ditch and ran towards it. I could hear Stipo urging me to go back but I didn't care. It was my little pet, as alive as could be.

'Maxie!' I shouted as I ran. 'Maxie, my little sweetie-pie!'

Chapter 8

'Maxie, little sweetie-pie!' I
shouted it again (I know it's
a dumb thing to say but that's how I talked to
her) and crouched down, clicking my fingers
for her to come.

Even in the dark I knew it was her, the
same way you know your own mom and dad
almost without looking. She cocked her head
on one side like she always did, one ear raised.

Even so, a thought flickered at the back of
my mind that there was something funny
about her. I forgot that the minute she started
gambolling towards me, because I was so
overjoyed.

But there was something wrong. She
dropped her nose to the ground which she
didn't usually do and somehow as she got
nearer she looked bigger and hairier. When

she was only a few yards away I could see long fangs and wild eyes and I knew there really was something wrong.

I was crouching with my arms held out to give her a big hug. She sprang towards me, not into my arms, but at my throat. In that last split second all I could see were frightening white fangs flecked with foam and crazed eyes as she sent me rolling over backwards.

She was bigger. She was hairier. She was so heavy she sent me flying and I could feel her breath like the air from a hot dungeon in my face and – far worse – these horrible teeth tearing at my waterproof where it was zipped up to the neck, as I tried to push her away.

Then she was gone.

As I scrambled up I saw what had happened. Stipo had grabbed her by the tail and was pulling her backwards as she turned and snapped at his hands. She was making the most terrifying snarling sounds – my timid little pup. Then I saw that Stodge had grabbed a branch from beneath the trees and was hitting her with it again and again.

'Don't hit her!' I couldn't stop myself shouting it because to me it still seemed as though they were beating my sweetie-pie.

As I was getting back on my feet, she came

again, growling and snarling, with her paws tearing at my chest as she tried to reach my throat. Then I saw why.

Stipo – incredibly – had let go of her so she was free to attack me again. 'Grab her!' I shouted as I tried to fend her off with my arms, and Stodge hit her again with the branch. Stipo had his hand inside his jacket, trying to find something.

And I could feel her long fangs ripping at my coat.

The next thing I saw was a flash of silver as Stipo held something above my face, right in front of the dog's eyes. Maxie stopped her frenzied snarling and slowly sank to the ground. Stipo moved round me and, bending down, advanced towards the dog, holding out what looked like a silver implement. Maxie growled low in her throat and began backing away, never taking her eyes off the flash of silver.

As he jabbed the silver forward towards her, Maxie spun around and fled, whimpering.

Stipo stood up and for the first time I could see what he was holding. It was a pair of kitchen scissors.

A pair of kitchen scissors, that was all. He was holding them in the open position. I just gaped.

'You okay?' Stodge asked, helping me up.

'I think so,' I gasped, but I was so shocked by what had happened that I really didn't know.

'Are you bleeding?' asked Stipo, peering at my throat. I ran my fingers round my neck. I couldn't feel any blood, although my water-proof was ripped. I shook my head, too numb to speak.

'Right,' he said, grabbing us both by the arms. 'Let's take a look over here.'

Several more windows in the big house were now lit up. Stipo ran stooping to the centre of the crossroads and I saw him pick something up. 'Now let's get out of here!' he said.

Chapter 9

We raced back through the wind and the rain, through the spooky wood, up the long hill, through bracken and heather. We ran and climbed and scrambled as best we could as though we were being pursued by demons, and perhaps in one sense we were. My legs ached and I could hardly breathe, but we kept on going, going, going.

We didn't speak – we didn't have enough breath, and anyway, I think we were all too scared by what we had seen.

As we hurtled down the moor at the back of the cottage, I could see the one lamp we'd left burning. I'd never been so glad to see a light in my life. We flung open the door, poured in, then Stodge slammed it behind us and closed all the locks and bolts.

We were safe.

For the moment.

I got out my flask of coffee and found some mugs in the kitchen. Stipo slumped on the floor and Stodge and I sat above him on the sofa, waiting to hear what he had to say.

Then Stipo showed us what he'd found. I ran to the bathroom to be sick.

He put it down on the floor between us. It was a red beret. A red beret stained with the darker red of blood.

The silence hung heavy in the low-ceilinged room. Then he spoke.

'Maxie is not dog any more, Lyddie.'

His dark brown eyes were fixed on mine, his black curly hair still wet from the rain.

'Maxie is now werewolf.'

'A werewolf?' I knew what he'd told us earlier about both people and dogs being turned into werewolves, and I knew that Chris Maultby had said Maxie had been bitten. But I couldn't bear to think my lovely little pet had suddenly become a ravening beast.

He hesitated before going on. 'Maxie is a werewolf.'

Stipo pushed himself up into a sitting position. 'Here you may laugh at such things, but my people know about them. We have werewolves there. They are more feared than . . .' he paused while he thought of the right word . . . 'more feared than Satan himself.'

'Is this how Count Lupus will rebuild his Empire of the Werewolves?' Stodge asked, sitting bolt upright.

'That's right,' Stipo said. 'Maxie is the first. There will be many others.'

The three of us sat there with the red beret on the floor between us.

I was almost too scared to ask, but I did. 'The beret . . . does that mean that poor little kid has been sacrificed?'

Stipo nodded. 'It takes a few days for a bitten dog to become a real werewolf – only a few hours for people. The sacrifice at the crossroads at midnight speeds it up. Tonight Maxie is only half werewolf. But sometimes they have sacrifices just for . . .'

He couldn't think of the word, but Stodge supplied it. 'Fun?' he said.

I looked at the bloodstained beret and thought about the grisly ritual at the crossroads. And about my little pet dog being slowly turned into a werewolf. It was too much to bear: Maxie had killed the child. Maybe – and I choked at the thought of it – she'd eaten it.

'What about the scissors?' Stodge asked.

'There are many legends about werewolves in my country, and there are stories of ways to defend yourself against them. They fear open scissors, although I do not think it would work on a full-grown werewolf.'

My turn next. 'Why is everyone so scared of them?'

He gave me a funny look. 'Why? Because they bite and turn others into werewolves like themselves. Because they destroy and kill. By day they may be as normal as us. At night they become killers, terrorizing everyone. They especially like to eat babies.'

Then he told us about Count Lupus. He had a castle in the refugees' country. There were many rumours and stories about his double life, and many people believed he was over three centuries old. That was why the refugees here were so alarmed when they heard he had also come to Britain. 'Here he will start a new reign of terror.'

Stodge clamped his podgy hands together and, in a not too sure voice, said, 'Let's just go and tell the police.'

Stipo shot him a scornful look. 'Would they believe us? Schoolkids with a wild story from a gypsy boy? They go to visit him and see a rich man in a big house with a grand car. They will say we are dreaming.'

'Perhaps we are,' said Stodge, with a confused, questioning look on his face.

At that moment we all froze. A spine-chilling howl echoed all around the cottage. It seemed to leak in through the windows and come down the chimney. On and on it went, then another long howl, then a third.

I switched the lamp off and we all crept over to the window. The moon was out in full, just peeping over the brow of the round moor. Against it, in perfect silhouette, we saw the shape of a big black wolf, its head raised to the skies as it poured out its dreadful music.

None of us could move. Finally, it lowered its head and disappeared back over the hill.

Stodge's hands were shaking. He didn't think he was dreaming now.

'Lupus?'

Stipo nodded.

'Does he know we're here?'

'If he knew, he'd be tearing at the door. Don't forget, we know what he is. He will have to destroy us.'

We all fell silent then, depressed at the thought of this demonic creature trying to hunt us down. It made me think of what my

mom had said when Dad lost all his money –
when he was cheated by his business partner –
and he was really down. 'Well,' she said, real
firm, 'you'll just have to get on and sort it out.
It's no use feeling sorry for yourself.'

So I said, 'Okay, so we hunt him down first.'

That cheered things up a bit. I went through
to the kitchen to boil the kettle for more coffee
and Stodge started fiddling with the radio.
When it came on – a local news programme –
it was so normal and everydayish that it
helped to break the spell of fear which was
gripping us.

'Plan of action,' I said, handing round the
steaming mugs. 'I'll find out everything I can
about the Count and Mawkworth Hall.'

Stodge liked the sound of this. 'And I'll do
some research on werewolves.' I thought he'd
be good at that: I remembered how clever he'd
been at finding the cottage.

'And somehow,' Stodge added, 'we've got to
get into the hall.' That sounded a bit scary but
at least we knew what we had to do now.

'That's better,' I said. 'We've got to get posi-
tive about this. The Count doesn't know where
we are, so we're safe here.'

Stodge put his finger to his lips and turned
up the radio. '. . .two cows found badly muti-

lated in fields in the Cheviots above Wooller, and several sheep killed over the past few weeks. Farmers are claiming that it is the Beast of Ackerford.'

We all knew what it meant, of course. Stodge sat nodding. 'See what a crafty chap this Count is. He's got everyone thinking it's the Beast of Ackerford.'

Chapter 10

It didn't seem right to disturb the beds upstairs (we were burglars, after all!) so we curled up like spoons on the floor, with me in the middle and the rug off the sofa over us. It was so cold. But once we'd snuggled up, me with my arms round Stipo, Stodge with his arms round me, we got warmed up (and no, Mom, there was nothing like that!). We were so tired, and the other two went out like a light, but I couldn't sleep.

All night, visions kept popping up in my head. Visions of Maxie tearing the flesh off a baby. It was horrible. By dawn I'd decided I just had to stop my imagination – rub out these thoughts like you'd erase something out of a schoolbook. And, for a while, I did.

The next morning we went down to the village to do what Stodge called 'our detective work'. We met up later at the Olde Tea-Shoppe in the square.

We all had loads of beans on toast with tea (for Stodge, natch) and coffee (for me and Stipo). And I felt kinda proud of my new buddies, or mates as they would say. Looking at the two of them, I realized how much I'd come to love and admire them in the few hours we'd been together. Bonding, I guess you'd call it.

Stipo, so quick and streetwise and brave. Stodge, so clever at working things out – I'd forgotten that he was really pretty brainy. He wouldn't let it show in school in case the other kids turned on him. We'd found out good stuff too.

Stodge said his piece first. He'd been to the library to check out werewolves and he'd even got on their computer and tapped into the Internet too. We listened to every word.

'Ly-can-thropy' – he spelt it out for us. That was the name for the way humans were turned into wolves. It went right back to the ancient Greeks to a guy called Lycaon who ate human flesh, which transformed him into a wolf.

Over the centuries, there were similar stories from almost every country in the world.

They were called *loupgarou* in France and *lobison* in Argentina and *vironsusi* in Finland, but they all meant the same thing – werewolf equals man-wolf.

According to the legends, there were several ways of becoming a werewolf. By being bitten, natch, by wearing a belt made from the tanned skin of an executed criminal, by drinking water from a wolf's paw print, by eating the roasted flesh of a rabid wolf . . . oh they went on and on, and they were all sick-making.

Stodge sat there with his eyes like saucers as he reeled them off. For protection, he said, there were the scissors that Stipo had used, or, if they came to get a sleeping child, it could be saved by having a nearby mirror reflecting the child's face as it slept. Again there were loads of them, and by the way Stipo sat nodding, he'd heard most of them before. 'By day they're humans, but at night they turn into wolves,' said Stodge. 'And if you wound the wolf, it still has the wound when it turns back into a man. Now for the worst bit,' said Stodge. 'In every country they say that werewolves eat babies and children.'

Around us the townspeople were pouring out their pots of tea and passing on the gossip: all we could think about then was that red beret. Stipo had put it into a paper bag and stuffed it through the letter-box of the police station.

But it wasn't any use thinking like that. 'That's terrific,' I said to Stodge. 'Now I've got some ace info for you.'

I'd pretended I was doing a school project on Mawkworth Hall, and, after asking around a bit, I'd been to see the local vicar who was also the local historian. He was a skinny old guy with white hair and he loved to talk.

Mawkworth Hall was, he'd told me, an unhappy story. It had been built by one of the mine-owners, who was famous for his cruelty – 'every stone built with our blood,' the miners said. The mine-owner had gone mad and killed his three children. And later there'd been another murder there. The locals shunned the place because they still thought it was haunted by its blood-stained past.

When I asked him who lived there now, he was quite helpful at first. It was a refugee from Eastern Europe, he said – no one was sure if he came from Bosnia or Latvia or Estonia, but it was one of those places. He appeared to have a lot of money.

He reckoned there were two other men with Count Lupus up at the hall. They didn't speak much English, but Count Lupus did and he regularly turned up at social events in the county. 'They say he is most charming,' the vicar said, but he said it in a way that suggested he didn't believe it.

When I asked if he liked him, he hesitated. 'There are stories . . . I know we shouldn't listen to rumours, and I know country people are superstitious, but even so. . .' His voice tailed off. He wasn't going to say any more.

Well, we sure knew more about werewolves than we did before. We ordered some toasted teacakes, more tea for Stodge and a coffee for me (why can't the English make proper coffee?).

We were just planning our next move when two women at the next table began talking about the missing children. One of them was reading bits out of the paper. We stopped talking and listened but we could only hear snatches.

'One of them was from the refugee camp down in Ackerford . . . poor little bairn. They say it's the Beast of Ackerford. I don't know . . . When I was young you never even needed to lock your door round here . . .' and so on and so on.

Then one of the women said she'd heard the

red beret had been handed in at the police station. 'No one knows who gave it in or where it was found . . . Let's hope they catch the man soon. They should do, they've called in police from all over the county, hundreds of them searching the area . . .'

The tea-shop was filling up with people coming in for lunch – or dinner as they called it round here – so we had to huddle round and speak quietly while we made our next plans. Stipo said he'd checked out the surrounding countryside that morning and found a quick way to get to the hall.

We went out into the square. It was a bright, cold, clear day. Everything looked so normal, with people doing their shopping and chatting, and it seemed impossible that we were on such a strange mission.

Until I spotted that big, black, sinister car, prowling along the road. I grabbed Stipo and Stodge by the arms and rushed all three of us into an alley. There, we watched as the car cruised to a halt just as one of the women who'd been at the next table in the tea-shop stepped on to the cobbles to cross the road. It was the Count, and – to my amazement – he looked as handsome as any film-star.

'I wonder if you'd be so kind as to help me,'

the Count said. He spoke beautiful English – posh English, as they say at my new school.

'What's the problem, hinny?' She leaned forward, her basket over her arm.

'We have some young people, aged around twelve or thirteen, staying at the Hall and they seem to have got lost. I wondered if you'd caught sight of them.'

He was no more than five yards away, but he hadn't seen us. My heart was in my mouth – the woman had been at the very next table.

'No, pet, not that I've seen,' she said. She'd been so busy gossiping she hadn't even noticed us.

'Thank you so much,' he said. He sat back in the seat and the car purred slowly off down the road.

Stipo had gone as white as candlefat and he wouldn't come out of the alley until the car was out of sight. 'He knows about us,' he hissed.

'Yep,' I said, 'but he didn't see us.'

We went back to the cottage, sneaking round the back so no one would see us, and we were just about to eat some sandwiches we'd picked up at the baker's when we heard the last sound in the world we'd expect. The doorbell.

Chapter 11

We all dived behind the sofa and looked at each other. No one knew we were here. At least, no one should know we were here. It rang again, two long rings. I went to try to peep but Stipo pulled me back down.

Who could it be?

There was a man's cough from outside the door, and the shape of a face at the window. One more long ring, then – with relief – we heard steps go down the path.

I was the first up. I peeped round the curtain. It was Count Lupus. Someone must have seen us at the cottage – and told him. Then the most amazing thing happened.

Just as though he knew we were there, he turned and faced the cottage and I had my first real good look at him.

To look at, he was a surefire hottie! Tall, slim, elegantly dressed in a slim-cut old-fashioned black suit, blue shirt and red silk tie, he had a great bod and his face . . . well, it was narrow and high-boned with the most amazing green eyes, and a thin confident smile. But for all that there hung about him an air of menace, an invisible cloud of danger; he was like a long thin dagger, beautiful but lethal.

I felt the other two pushing behind me and none of us could tear our eyes away as we watched what happened next. The Count opened his jacket. Around his waist I could see a thick leather belt with a heavy iron buckle, hanging undone.

Smiling at the house, just as though he was smiling at us, he took the two halves of the buckle and fastened them together. There was a roaring sound, like huge waves, but I knew it was only in our heads – no one else would hear it.

The Count seemed to grow bigger. Hair began to sprout from beneath his sleeves all over his hands. Then I looked at his face and watched the great sprouts of thick hair growing down the sides, over his cheeks, everywhere except on those green eyes which glowed through the mass of black and silver hair. He was a huge, beautiful and terrifying wolf.

At the same time, the sky darkened as though before a storm. It was like dusk, but we could still make out the figure by the gate. He lifted his head and gave a growl that echoed right around the house, and then turned into a howl that seemed to shrivel my bones. As he howled, I could see the long, white, vicious fangs. All three of us were frozen in our pose behind the curtain.

Then, so quickly I hardly saw it, he unbuckled the belt. Instantly the hair and fangs vanished. He was a man again.

He stood there for a moment, looking at the cottage and smiling his deadly dagger smile. Then, as though nothing had happened, he turned and got in his car and drove gently off. It was hard to believe what we'd seen. But as soon as he had gone, we all began jabbering – pure fear!

'I forgot to tell you,' said Stodge, his teeth chattering as he tried to speak. 'Lupus means wolf.'

'That belt,' Stipo said, and his hands were trembling. 'It's the veronshika. It's made from the skin of a murderer and it can turn you into a werewolf.'

'Never mind that,' I said, practically gibbering. 'Does he know we are in the house?'

Stipo's dark eyes met mine. 'Of course. He was showing us what he can do.'

Stodge tried to put a brave face on. 'Still, he went away, didn't he?'

'Yes,' I said, cheering up a bit, 'he didn't try anything, did he?'

A weary look of sadness touched Stipo's face. 'Night-time. That is the time of the werewolf.'

After that, no one knew what to say. So Stodge switched on the radio for a bit of music to make the cottage less frightening and, sure enough, on the news bulletin there it was . . . a third child had gone missing. We had to do something. But now it was all different: we thought we'd been hunting him, but he was hunting us.

Chapter 12

Huddled together in the cottage, we waited for night-time – the time of the werewolf. We knew he'd come back, but, after seeing that terrifying display of his power – turning into a wolf before our eyes – we were paralysed by fear. We could all feel the sense of menace building around us. We were getting nearer and nearer to the heart of all this evil and now it seemed to be touching us.

The only thing that kept me going was being together. These were my two mates. They were the best thing to happen to me since our family disaster and I loved them both.

With the light out, we curled up again, spoon-style, like we had the night before, with me in the middle and the two boys on either side. Before we settled down, Stipo took the mirror off the mantelpiece and put it beside us. At our feet he placed a bunch of rosemary he'd picked up somewhere. It would make us safe, he thought.

After all the things that had happened, I thought anything was worth a try.

Strangely I fell instantly into a deep sleep – probably shock, I guess. I dreamed I was back in our old Kent farmhouse with Mom and Dad and Maxie and we were watching Harry Enfield on television. We'd all loved Harry Enfield, and we were all roaring with laughter by the warmth of the fire, and all was serene and happy.

Then there was the most terrible crashing sound and Harry's friendly face suddenly turned . . . into a wolf! My happy dream had become a nightmare.

I was sitting up and screaming before I realized it wasn't a dream or a nightmare. Crouching a yard away, mouth gaping, long fangs gleaming, red tongue lolling among dripping white foam, was a huge wolf. Its feet were braced, ready to leap.

Behind the wolf the rear window was shattered where it had leapt through.

I screamed and screamed, panic rolling through my mind in waves. I couldn't even think, I was so shaken by fear.

Then I remembered I wasn't alone. Stipo and Stodge were both hugging me, we were all hugging each other, locked in terror before this frightening spectacle.

'Stay still,' Stipo whispered. I realized why. We were all reflected in the mirror he'd put beside us. Three chalk-white faces, eyes popping. That was the only thing stopping the wolf leaping upon us and tearing us to pieces.

It hunkered back on its haunches, giving out one fierce growl after another. Its eyes, a vivid green, were ringed with red circles. It wriggled on its haunches, wanting to pounce but held back by that mirror image. The long white flesh-piercing teeth snapped in anger. Around its neck I saw a collar with an iron buckle – the same buckle I'd seen on the belt. I knew then for sure. This was Count Lupus. Come for his final revenge.

'Steady!' Stipo muttered. He leaned forward, still clinging to me. His free hand was scrabbling about on the floor. What was he playing at? At least Stodge had a good idea. He'd reached up to the table and got hold of a carving knife.

With one desperate lunge, Stodge swung the knife in a huge arc. The wolf drew back but the knife caught the edge of one front paw. Its vast black head was raised and its mouth was open like a cavern as it gave a roar like a dragon.

It wasn't frightened. It was enraged.

Stodge dropped the knife and came shivering back to me.

Stipo had found what he was looking for. It was the bunch of rosemary. He let go of me and slowly inched forward on his hands and knees, straight toward the growling beast which stood before us. He held out the rosemary.

If a big knife didn't frighten it, what the hell did he think he was doing with a bunch of herbs?

Another inch forward. Pushed out the rosemary. Another inch. He was only six inches away from those foaming fangs.

Slowly, the wolf backed off, growling ferociously.

He edged nearer, holding the rosemary in front of him. The wolf moved back again, snapping in rage as it did so.

Then Stipo kneeled up and jabbed the spiky herb straight at the beast's face.

It leapt back this time. Then it raised its fearsome head and gave a howl that filled the room, that seemed to fill the universe with fear and terror. It shook my bones and turned my heart around. And just when it seemed there was no end but death, it spun around, leapt through the shattered window and was gone.

We collapsed into each other's arms, shaking with a hysterical mix of fear and relief. We were alive!

Stipo explained it all as we calmed down. He was afraid that if we moved about too much our image would disappear from the mirror and then we would be at the mercy of the werewolf. He'd heard from his people that werewolves could not bear the scent of the rosemary bush. But he didn't know for sure. No one knew for sure. And I hugged my brave boy who'd saved us all.

But it was Stodge, the practical one, who pointed out we couldn't stay there. Lilac Cottage would never be a safe haven again. We gathered together our things and left quietly. We trudged wearily over the moors, keeping to the shadow of the old stone walls and avoiding the high ground.

After two hours' walking, we found a wood. Within a few minutes Stipo had built a shelter of branches. He lit a small fire of twigs by the entrance and soon it was warm and cosy. We curled up again, the rosemary at our feet, a soft night breeze rustling the leaves around us. Strangely, I felt very safe here.

Quietly we sat round the fire and worked out what to do next. It was Stodge who saw it most clearly. 'We've got to attack – we can't let him hunt us down. We'll go into Mawkworth Hall and face him.'

'We must,' Stipo agreed. 'There are still two little kids to save.'

He was right. One had been sacrificed at the crossroads, but there were still two – presumably alive.

'Okay,' I said. 'But first thing tomorrow we've got to get back to Ackerford and see PC Squires. We're gonna need help.'

'Will he believe you?' the gypsy boy asked.

'He sure has to,' I replied. But in my heart I wasn't half as confident as I sounded.

Chapter 13

Early the next morning, before the mists had lifted, we were down by the roadside, thumbing. By luck, the first vehicle to pass – a cattle wagon heading to market – gave us a lift.

Along the way we passed several police cars, even at that time of day. 'Out hunting the Beast of Ackerford', said the farmer. He wasn't joking; by now everyone was taking it seriously.

Andy Squires was having his breakfast when his wife let us in. She gave us cups of tea, while he polished off his bacon, pushed his chair back, and sat listening to our story. His big meaty face looked sober and concerned as we talked.

'Do you believe us?' I asked, when we got to the end.

He stirred his tea and looked me straight in the eye. 'I do, hinny,' he said. 'Chris Maultby's got the report from the lab. Your little pup had wolf's blood in her. Anyway, you still hear stories up in the hills here about the time – hundreds of years ago, mind – when wolves roamed the land. There were werewolves here too, according to legend. And we've got to save those two kiddies. No, I don't laugh at folklore. The problem is, what do we do about it?'

Then he began questioning Stipo about his knowledge of werewolves.

Stipo, who'd saved us with crossed scissors, mirrors and even rosemary, told him that the only other thing he knew was that werewolves were afraid of St Hubert – that was why he'd been pleased to see our local church was St Hubert's. 'I think he was patron saint of hunters – something like that,' he said.

'Right,' said the cop, standing up and putting on his jacket. 'I'll give the Rev. Stedham a ring to see what he can tell us.' He went out to use the telephone in the hall, and when he came back he said the vicar would see us all now – urgently!

'We need all the weapons we can get,' I said, meaning all the knowledge we could gather about werewolves. But that made PC Squires think. He paused.

'Good idea,' he said, and went into the back porch. When he came out he was loading bullets into the magazine of a rifle. 'We're going nowhere without my old chum here.'

I saw Stipo give a sad little shake of the head and I knew what he meant. Guns are no good against a creature that cannot die.

The village was deathly quiet. I knew all the kids would be in school, but even so you'd think a plague had hit the place. Over the level crossing, past the village hall, it was all deserted. Even the three shops looked empty.

It was dark too. Huge thunderheads of black clouds had rolled across the sky. It looked as though the world was coming to an end. The more I looked at the clouds, the more I thought they looked like a huge wolf's head, towering above us. I closed my eyes and shook my head, but when I opened them the clouds still looked the same. I knew I was hallucinating, but I still felt the coldness of fear in my veins.

PC Squires was marching ahead of us three and as he turned into Church Lane, he stopped in his tracks. I looked up and saw why.

In the middle of the road, in broad daylight, was a werewolf! I knew – and don't ask me how – that it was Maxie (or what had been Maxie) and not Count Lupus.

Between its front paws was what looked like a pile of white firewood. As the werewolf saw us, it lifted its head, stared at us, and its rumbling growl filled the silent street. It was huge and – in a strange way – almost beautiful. It was twice the size of the biggest dog, its thick shaggy coat as black as soot, its eyes rolling white.

All three of us clung together behind the big policeman, frozen by terror. Suddenly the ordinary world had turned once again into a nightmare. Then, that sound again: the howl from hell ringing and echoing all around as the wolf lifted its great head and roared to the dark skies.

PC Squires reeled back. He'd never heard it before and it shook him badly. Even so, he gathered himself, pushed us behind him, and, talking to himself, muttered, 'Right, you devil, see how you like this lot.'

Deliberately, he lifted the gun to his shoulder and took careful aim. At that distance, about 20 yards, he couldn't miss. But the werewolf only lifted its great head and howled again.

'Hell!' said Andy Squires. 'That should've done it. Okay – second go.'

He lifted the gun, took aim even more carefully, and again squeezed the trigger.

The werewolf shook its head as though pestered by flies. This time the howl was a cry of triumph and slowly it began to move towards us. Andy Squires lowered the gun and stared in disbelief. His weapon was useless against this death-defying beast, and we were powerless to move.

It was Stodge who broke the spell. 'Quick – up here!' There was a narrow alley behind the back of the bank which led to the churchyard and Stodge had turned and was running up it. We all followed, scrambling along as fast as we could.

Only a few more yards to go! I took a quick glance backwards and saw the werewolf pacing after us, a silver slaver hanging down like lace from its open red mouth – and the curve of the white fangs.

Up the three stone steps, Andy Squires kicked open the rusty old iron gate and shoved us through it before he dived through himself. He slammed the iron bolt across just as the monstrous beast flung itself at the gate. Its gleaming teeth grazed his fingers as he snatched his hand back. Then he put his big arms around us and pulled us together, panting and fearful, as we watched to see what would happen.

The werewolf pulled back. It looked at the church wall – it was only about four-feet high. It could easily jump that. And we had nowhere else to run.

Could St Hubert – whoever he was – save us?

For the werewolf had pulled back on to its haunches and was ready to leap.

Chapter 14

In that awful silence, I heard a strange chanting. At first I wondered what it was.

I looked over my shoulder and coming out of the church door was the Rev. Stedham – he was a young, baby-faced sort of vicar – marching slowly, steadily towards us.

He was holding a three-foot crucifix in his right hand and a book in his left. And what he was reading aloud sounded like a Latin prayer.

On and on he went, marching purposefully and all the time proclaiming in his high boyish voice. He came up to us and we parted to let him through. Then he walked right up to the narrow gate still reciting his sing-song prayer.

The werewolf fell back. The vicar pulled back the iron bolt and the gate opened with a squeak. There was nothing between him and the snarling beast now – except his crucifix and his prayer-book.

We all stood and watched in horror as he walked towards the werewolf, his eyes on the prayer-book, his voice perfectly steady. When he was a yard away, the crouching wolf shuffled back, then back again as the clergyman kept moving forward.

Rev. Stedham finished the prayer. He closed the prayer-book. Then he lowered the crucifix and pointed it straight at the werewolf.

It spun in the dust and fled. Faster than any deer, it shot down the alley and we could hear its howls – this time howls of despair – it ran through the town and out on to the moors.

It was defeated.

A few minutes later, still shaking, we were having cups of tea in the vestry. The vicar explained that, after the policeman had telephoned, he had just had time to look up an ancient prayer in one of his theological books. What did it say, we all asked.

'Let's just say that it brings down the power of the Lord on Satan and all his works,' he said, with a quiet smile.

For such a mild guy with a squeaky voice, he certainly seemed to have plenty of guts.

'Well, your prayers worked a lot better than my rifle,' PC Squires said.

'Well, of course, this church is named after St Hubert,' said the vicar. 'The legend says that werewolves are terrified of the saint. I've never had occasion to test it before, but it certainly seemed to work today.'

To be honest, it had all set me thinking that in the past I'd never bothered too much about church and all that stuff, but I'd pay more attention to it in the future.

'Do you know much about the folklore?' Andy Squires asked him.

'A little,' said the young vicar. 'When I was coming here, I read up on it. And of course your rifle wouldn't work – according to the old legends, werewolves can deflect ordinary bullets.'

'Is right,' Stipo said. 'You cannot shoot werewolf.'

'So what do we do?' Andy Squires looked helpless.

'Well,' the vicar went on, 'if I remember correctly, and I think I do, the only thing that can kill a werewolf is a silver bullet.'

'Is right,' Stipo said, excitedly. 'Silver bullet can kill werewolf.'

'I hope young Stodge is all right,' the

policeman suddenly said. Stodge had gone out to make sure the werewolf had gone, although we had heard its howling progress as it headed for the hills.

At that moment, our fat pal burst through the door. He was pale and panting and looked as though he wanted to be sick. He was holding a handkerchief in his hands.

'Look,' he said. He put the hanky on the table and slowly opened it. We all leaned forward. There spread out on the table was what I'd taken to be white firewood (never questioning why a werewolf would want to chew firewood).

Bones. They were small, fine bones. Too big for a chicken. To small for a dog.

They were human.

The bones of a child.

Arms, legs, ribs, suddenly I could recognize each and every one. The skull, splintered across the top with chewing, stared up at us with empty, aching eye sockets.

What had once been my pet Maxie had been chewing up the bones of one of the missing children.

I bolted for the loo with my hand over my mouth.

We'd been saved yet again, this time by the

vicar with his prayers. But another child had died, another was still missing, and how many more were to disappear?

When I returned, the cop had bundled up the bones and put them away.

When you looked at them, you just couldn't think.

'So what now?' PC Squires said. He looked sombre and depressed. There seemed to be no answers.

'Silver bullets,' said Stipo. 'We must have silver bullets.'

'I'm afraid you won't find much silver in this town,' the vicar replied. 'There's not much money in Ackerford, I'm afraid.'

Stipo leaned forward, eyes blazing. 'There are my people.'

'But the gypsies . . .' Stodge began to say, then stopped himself.

'You don't have any money, surely,' the cop said.

But Stipo was unstoppable. 'You do not understand. My people do not trust banks, so they put what little they have into gold and silver – mostly silver. That is the tradition.'

'All right,' said the policeman, 'but why would a gypsy want to help?'

Stipo's quick glance took in all of us.

'Because you have been afraid for a few hours. We have been afraid for five hundred years. We fear the Empire of the Werewolves.'

Chapter 15

Stipo took from his pocket a magnificent silver cigarette case. For a brief moment he gazed at it, then, giving himself a little shake, he handed it over to PC Squires, 'It was my grandfather's.' He paused. 'But how do we get it made into bullets?'

'I think we can manage that,' said PC Squires. 'I've rung Chris Maultby on my mobile and he's got the forge to open up – and we're going back to the church too.'

The church? Why return there? Anyway, at the forge, we three waited in the car while the policeman and vet went inside. We could hear the roar of the fire and see the sparks and bursts of yellow and orange flames. Eventually they both came out and Chris

Maultby showed us what he'd got wrapped in an oily cloth.

Two dirty silver bullets, slightly smaller than the lid of a biro.

That was all we had to fight the werewolves. Somehow, in that oily cloth, it didn't look enough.

'There was only enough for two,' said Chris. 'But never mind, Andy, you're a pretty good shot when it comes to rabbits.'

'Aye, but they're not leaping at you trying to rip your throat out,' said the policeman, lifting his rifle out of the boot. ' Still, with two, it allows me one miss.'

'No,' I yelled. 'No, it doesn't. That wasn't Count Lupus back there. That was Maxie. There's two of them. You'll need two silver bullets, and two good shots.'

'Damn,' he said. 'You're right.'

We all went quieter then. Everything seemed to be going so well that we'd almost forgotten the task that lay before us. Two werewolves, two bullets. That was it.

'First, St Hubert's,' said Chris Maultby.

Apparently the vicar had said that if we had the gun and bullets blessed at the church it would give them more power. It was all legend and folklore now, but that was all we had on our side. We had to believe in it. And, after all, the vicar's Latin prayer had sure scared the werewolf off earlier.

The young vicar was waiting for us. It was a weird kinda service. The vicar, a baby-faced young guy, placed the rifle and the bullets on the altar, knelt before them and prayed. We did the same.

I can't remember what he said, except he told us afterwards it was something else he'd found in one of his old books. One bit made me shiver. 'When Satan comes in the wolf's coat, to devour our babes and lay waste the world, please you God to come to our aid . . .'

Afterwards, Stipo picked up the gun and expertly began to slot the two bullets into the magazine. When Andy Squires reached to take it off him, he simply said: 'I know about guns.'

Silently we trooped out of the church and stood together on the path. I shivered. It was getting cold.

'We've done everything we can,' said Chris Maultby, in his sensible, crisp voice. 'Let's get on with it. Mawkworth Hall, here we come.'

'Don't forget,' Stodge said, 'there's still one child left. We may still be in time to save it.'

And it was good to feel that we were once again the hunters. But we were armed only with two bullets made from gypsies' silver. Would they work?

Silence reigned in the car as we sped on our way.

Chapter 16

Mawkworth Hall looked like a Hollywood set. Huge arc lights in the road lit up the entire building, and I'd never seen so many policemen in all my life. Andy Squires had been on his mobile to headquarters and they'd switched all the men hunting the Beast of Ackerford to the Hall.

There were police cars and ambulances all along the roadside, dozens of uniformed officers in groups in the road, and around the tall wrought iron gates there were paramilitaries crouching, automatic rifles trained on the house. The ugly Gothic turrets of the Hall stood ragged and black against the light. It was a siege.

As we got out, PC Squires was immediately called over to a tall figure in a fancy uniform decked out with lots of extra braid – one of those straight-backed, born-to-command guys, you know – and they huddled together and spoke for some time before he came back to us.

He looked so desperately worried and afraid that I felt real sorry for him. But there wasn't a hint of anxiety in his voice. 'The Chief Constable's taking my advice – well, Stipo's really. They've got loudspeakers but there's to be no offer of a surrender. We've got to shoot them down . . .' He didn't finish. Count Lupus and Maxie were mad dogs really.

'Gimme the gun,' he said. He pulled a wry face. 'Not that the Chief Constable was very impressed with our theory of silver bullets – he's got more faith in his own firepower.'

'I'll come in with you, Andy,' said Chris Maultby, and I admired him for that.

The cop wasn't having any of it. 'This is my job, thank you, Chris. And I'll look after it. You kids, wait here by the gate and I'll blow my whistle when it's sorted.'

'Good luck,' said Stodge, a weak kinda voice. All our hearts were in our mouths as the policeman pushed his way through the professional snipers with his rifle under his arm. They fell apart to let him through. As he moved to open the gates, one of the paramilitary cops held him back. 'Wait,' he said, so our Ackerford policeman stood there, his gun under his arm.

We didn't have to wait long. Right on cue, the massive front door of the house creaked open. Out stepped . . . the werewolf. Maxie.

It stood on the step, its head held proudly high, its thick black coat shining in the lights, and delivered a howl that seemed to tear the black skies apart. The murmuring and fidgeting of the men stopped instantly. A dozen or more rifles were steadily trained on the wicked, beautiful creature.

Then it dropped its head to pick up something – I couldn't see what – in its jaws and trotted down the steps and over the gravelled drive towards the gate and PC Squires.

When it was three yards from the gate it stopped and dropped what it had been chewing. Then it picked it up in its jaws and threw it in the air. It landed a yard away from my nose, where I was crouched by the gates.

It was the torn remains of a baby.

Gross! I nearly threw up there and then, and turned my face away before daring to look again. I could see a complete arm and half a dimpled leg hanging from the ripped-up torso. It was the third youngster. We were too late.

Even the police marksmen fell back from the horror of this sight, and in triumph the werewolf lifted its head and howled again and again, the night ringing with its haunting cries.

The voice of the Chief Constable was crisp and clear in the night air. 'Fire at random.'

The clicking and cocking of firearms was followed by a burst of shots, some single, some streams of automatic fire. All around the werewolf the bullets kicked up the dirt and made the gravel dance. On and on it went, faster and louder, and the werewolf – which must have been hit by a hundred bullets – never flinched.

Slowly the shooting petered out. It was no good. They couldn't hurt it. Nothing could hurt it . . . except perhaps our silver bullets.

In the silence which followed there was a buzz of voices from around the Chief Constable. Then he called out again. 'Let Squires through.'

One of the marksmen pushed open the creaking gates and Andy Squires stepped through on to the gravel, a few yards away from where the werewolf stood gnawing its grisly prize.

All these men, all this firepower, and in the end it came down to a village bobby with his old rifle. It was our only hope of preventing centuries of horror.

The wolf seemed oblivious to him at first. It picked up the remains of the child, gave one bite so tremendous that I could see the blood burst out of the almost-severed leg, and dropped it again on the gravel. A dog playing with a bone.

Then it turned to face Andy, the blood bright on its white fangs, its eyes flashing murderously in the lights, and sprang.

Even with the gates protecting us, me and Stodge and Stipo – and some of the cops – reeled backwards as this horrible spectacle came hurtling through the air.

But Andy Squires never flinched. He'd dropped into a kneeling position to steady his aim and was pointing the rifle straight at the wolf. There was one dull crump of a sound and the flying wolf, mouth agape and growling viciously, landed on him, its mouth hunting his throat.

No one moved. We were powerless. We were about to see a man torn to death and we couldn't lift a finger to help.

Andy was lying on his back with the beast sprawled across him. It wasn't moving. The growling and roaring had stopped. Only silence now, as it lay across him like a film-star's fur coat. He wasn't moving either. We watched, hardly daring to breathe.

Then, with a grunt, the policeman pushed himself up, and the weight of the werewolf slid off him, and fell to the gravel completely life-less. In the centre of its forehead was a hole where the silver bullet had entered. It had worked. It was dead.

We cheered, every one of us, we cheered our brave cop with his old-fashioned gun, and we cheered the dead body of the beast that seconds before had held us all in thrall. 'One down,' said Andy Squires, 'one to go.'

And he set off, his feet crunching on the gravel as he walked towards the house.

Two paramilitary guys pulled the gates open and began to put the child's remains into a white bag. Ghoulish as it was, I couldn't take my eyes off it. When they stood up, I heard one of them exclaim: 'Hell, take a look at that!'

He was pointing at the body of the werewolf. Only it wasn't a werewolf any more. It had shrunk to the tiny comical short-legged body of a dachshund. Maxie, the dead Daxie.

Chapter 17

One down, one to go. That was what he'd said. We all watched in silent admiration as PC Squires, village bobby, a portly middle-aged man who should be bouncing grandchildren on his knee, walked up to that door, pushed it open with the rifle, and vanished inside.

All these modern cops, trained in fighting terrorists and international criminals, armed with the latest high-tech weapons, could only watch as he entered the werewolf's lair.

Suddenly I thought watching wasn't good enough. We'd been right up at the sharp end all along and we weren't going to miss out now.

I tugged at Stipo's sleeve and caught Stodge's eye and we edged through the crowd to the darkness of the road.

'Let's go help him,' I said, as Stipo emerged.

'I go,' he said, and the three of us set off creeping around the high stone walls. We found the two back gates, but both were guarded by policemen who shooed us away. Finally we found a part of the wall that was covered in ivy. Stipo went up first. 'Fine, follow me.'

I helped Stodge up and then followed.

Without even looking, we skittered down a grassy bank, across a paved area and up to the back of the house. It was totally black here, away from the lights. I found a narrow door and one by one we all went through. A breath of cold damp wind brushed our faces. The heavy door slammed shut behind us.

We were in the lair of the werewolf! And boy, were we scared!

With me first (you know I'm kinda bossy) we crept up the corridor in front of us. This, I reckoned, should lead us to the front door and maybe we'd find PC Squires there.

The stone walls were cold and hard to my fingers as I stumbled along. One corner, then another, and boy, was it creepy.

Next we were in a big hall. The light from the lamps outside slanted through the gaps in the shuttered windows just enough to make the shadows dance. On the walls were animal heads, around the edges of the room huge chunks of dark furniture. Our feet scraped on the stone floor.

No sign of the cop. Had he gone out again? Somewhere here was the door he'd come in. I felt along the wall until I found it, and the big iron lock. No key. Gone.

Then I was really scared. Motioning to the other two, I stumbled back down the corridor to the door where we'd come in. That key had gone too.

We were locked in the lair of the werewolf.

The voice made all of us nearly jump out of our skins. It echoed along the corridors and halls, bouncing off the cold stone, a jeering, teasing, cruel voice. It was the Count.

'Welcome!' the voice said. 'Welcome to my guests. Welcome to the gypsy brat, the girl who is as stupid as most Americans, and the fat boy, and welcome to the policeman.'

He was talking as though he had all the time in the world. Perhaps he had. By now we'd crept back up to the hall and – I'm not ashamed to admit it – all three of us were clinging together. All we could do was wait.

'You want to play games with the great Count Lupus, king of the werewolves? Very well, come and play hide-and-seek . . .' And it

ended with a laugh that was full of charm –
and even more full of horror. He'd got us now.

I felt Stipo's arm tighten round my waist and
Stodge's hand freeze in mine. My mouth was so
dry it was like wood, my heart was leaping in
my chest, and my brain had turned to cotton
wool. I was so scared I couldn't even think.

Slowly, as though mesmerized, we moved
towards that taunting, welcoming voice. It was
coming from behind another of the wooden
panelled doors.

'Come, my guests,' said the voice again.

As our eyes adjusted to the half-light, I
could see another of the wooden panelled doors
was ajar. Gently, I pushed it. With a creak, it
swung open, and Stodge, Stipo and me stood in
the doorway.

There was just enough light creeping
through the casement windows for us to see
the room pretty clearly. It was a long dining
hall, like the ones you see in old films: high
arched stone ceiling, pillars around the walls,
old armour and paintings, and in the middle a
great table set with silver for a banquet. In
this light, everything looked silver and black.

I took all this in at a glance because my gaze
went straight to the figure standing on what
looked like a raised stage at the far end of the

room. It was Count Lupus. He looked . . . sort of splendid.

I say splendid for there really was a sort of evil glory about him. He looked even taller. On his head was an enormous fur hat and a fur coat reached from his shoulders to the ground. His handsome face, lit by a cruel smile, radiated strength. He was the master. He knew it, and so did we.

'As you see,' he said, with a gesture towards the table, 'tonight I shall feast like a king. A three-course dinner, I think.'

And we knew what the three courses were. Us.

His eyes flicked beyond us. 'And perhaps with some older, tougher meat later,' he said.

I looked back. PC Squires had come through the door. My heart sank. Instead of coming to our rescue, he was looking completely bemused. Mouth half open, he looked around the museum of a room, then at the figure on the stage and he too moved forward as though in a dream.

It was all so unreal, so unearthly. With this room like a scene out of history and this arrogant man acting like a god, our cop seemed to have lost that down-to-earth grit that had seen him through so far.

Truth is, he looked like a real old guy.

Nothing could save us now. I remembered the other werewolf and how it had chewed the child's limbs and I felt crippled with fear. That's what would happen to us.

Chapter 18

'So this is the army they have sent against me.' His words were mocking. This was how he was going to torture us before we felt his fangs on our flesh.

'Three impudent young people, one old man! Yet I shall bring you to glory, a glory beyond your dreams. Tonight you will join the brotherhood of the Werewolves. Eternal life will be yours. We shall taste child-flesh together and run through the woods side by side. The world will be ours. The old empire will be restored.'

It was just as Stipo had said. The Empire of the Werewolves – when wickedness ruled the world – was coming to life again. And we were to be part of it.

All the time we had shuffled nearer, drawn by that hypnotic voice. I seemed to have no will left of my own. But Stodge had, and it was

Stodge who half-turned to Andy Squires, standing just behind us, and yelled: 'Shoot him! Shoot him now!'

Andy Squires looked at the gun beneath his arm as though he had never seen it before. Stodge grabbed it and pushed it into his hands.

'Now!' he urged.

As we all watched, he lifted it slowly in his hands, as though he only dimly remembered what it was. His hands were shaking. He wouldn't even be able to hit the wall in that state. Then, miraculously, his hands steadied. I saw him take aim and his finger curl around the trigger.

Silence.

'He can't!' The Count, who had not even bothered to move, gave his melodious, hateful laugh.

This time it was Stipo's turn. He shook the policeman's arm. 'Now! Shoot while he's standing still! Quick!'

Slowly, PC Squires lowered the gun. He shook his head, slowly, sadly, a baffled look on his face. 'He's right. I canna shoot a man. I canna shoot another human being.'

'But he's not,' Stipo hissed. 'He's not a man. He's a werewolf!'

When the Count spoke again, his voice was low with menace. The charm had gone. 'Perhaps this will make it easier for him. You shall see again the miracle of transformation. Then you will feel the fangs that will be your salvation before you too join the brotherhood of wolfmen.'

He straightened himself up, a towering figure, and opened the wolfskin robe. I saw the belt I had seen before. His elegant slim fingers took the open buckle and fastened it with a loud click.

We all knew what would come next. He was changing into a werewolf.

Then our turn would come.

We couldn't take our eyes off him. We couldn't speak. We couldn't move.

First I saw his upheld hands darken as the hair sprouted. It seemed to gush from his cuffs and his long slim fingers turned into hooked claws.

His eyes went slittier and even greener, so they shone in the half-dark, and his smile turned to a vengeful display of long white fangs, until his tongue – blood red – hung slavering over them.

By then he had a wolf's head. The wolfskin hat and cloak seemed to fit around his body and become part of him, so that within seconds this princely figure was a massive wolf, raised on its back legs, its front paws paddling the air.

Even though I knew we were all going to die a terrible death, even though I knew we would then take terror with us wherever we went, even though fear coursed through my veins, I still saw him as a magnificent, kingly creature. That was the most frightening thing of all.

Did I really want his promise of eternal glory?

Before I could think again, the wolf sprang from the stage on to the table.

Cutlery and plates slid around and crashed to the floor. No one gave them a glance. We couldn't take our eyes off this mighty beast.

It was two, or three times, bigger than the one we'd seen outside. His bushy coat was black dashed with majestic streaks of silver. Standing in the middle of that table, he raised his head and the howl was like none I'd heard before. It was a high proud howl, followed by another and another until the howling flooded the room, filled the house and seemed to burst out and echo all around the universe. There was nothing left in the world but these howls from hell. My bones turned to jelly. My brain broke into a thousand pieces.

Werewolf

There was a clatter on the floor just behind me. The cop was so dazed he'd dropped the gun. Not that it mattered any more, for the werewolf, its green eyes now ringed with red, was hunkering down, ready to leap.

Did I want to feel its fangs on my throat? Did I want to be reborn to rule the world?

But it wasn't coming for me. It landed just in front of Andy Squires, rose on its back legs and put its long-clawed paws on his shoulders, towering over him. It growled right into his face so that the silver slaver dripped down the front of his uniform.

Poor old Andy reeled backwards against the stone wall, and slumped to the ground. He might have been dead by the way he lay there.

Instinctively, we ran. Me and Stodge down one side of the table, Stipo down the other.

But it was no good. There was no escape. The werewolf turned from the slumped policeman and leapt back on to the table, skidding the whole length of it. Then he leapt off again and ran among us, between the table legs and the chairs, in and out, round and round, snarling viciously all the time.

I couldn't keep track of where it was. One second it was flashing past Stipo knocking him to the ground, the next I could feel its teeth snapping at my clothes, its hot breath stinking like a grave.

We ran again, twisting and turning, but wherever we went it was there, tripping our feeble legs as we screamed and ran and scrambled. All was madness and pandemonium. I felt its teeth again, on my arm this time, and screamed. But the skin wasn't broken.

It didn't mean to break the skin.

This was the game; werewolf hide-and-seek. This was the terror we must endure before he finally ripped out our throats and took us into his cruel brotherhood.

Suddenly it stopped. It stood quite still in the centre of the table. It raised its ferocious head and gave one last howl that was more like a lion's roar. This was it. Now it was ready to take us into the brotherhood.

Chapter 19

I was cowering down under the table, just peeping over the top. Stodge was clinging to one of the carved table legs, and Stipo was somewhere over by the stage. We could run no more.

It loped easily off the end of the table and padded towards me. I was to be the first. It placed one paw on my chest, easily pushing me down to the floor. As its face came closer, I could see the Count's eyes quite clearly amongst the black and silver fur. The evil shone as brightly as the green.

As the cruel fangs glided over my throat, ready to open the soft flesh, I could smell the blood of children on its breath. I closed my eyes and tried to remember a prayer.

Instead came a furious snarling. I opened my eyes. Andy Squires was trying to save me.

He was standing with a chair in his hands, thrashing the back of the werewolf.

An old man, beaten by forces he didn't understand, staging one last rally to try to save us.

The werewolf rose once more to its back feet, locked its mighty jaws over the leg of the chair and tore it contemptuously from his weak grasp. With a toss of its head, it flung the chair across the room.

Beneath the weight of its paws, the policeman sank to the ground. He was going to be the first to die.

One snap of the fangs ripped away his tie and collar. Another, and his throat was laid bare. The werewolf, with the old guy pinned beneath him, gave one last rumbling growl and went for his throat with a swift movement.

Choking down a cry, all I could do was to turn my head away. I couldn't bear to see a good man die.

The crump sound was kinda muffled, but I recognized it. I spun back. The werewolf had backed off and was shaking its head as though puzzled. It tried to spring on to the table but for some reason it was now too weak and could only clamber feebly up on to it.

There, it swayed, took a few staggering steps,

and crashed on to its side. In the centre of its chest, a ragged blood-soaked hole scarred its fur.

Stodge was kneeling on the floor, blinking stupidly. In his hands was the gun. Just as it was about to take its first victim, good old Stodge had picked up the gun and shot it.

He dropped the gun and panting through his open mouth, shuffled over to look at the werewolf. As he reached out one hand to touch, I heard Stipo shriek: 'Don't touch it!' But it was too late.

As Stodge's trembling hand hung in the air, the werewolf raised its head, opened its eyes, and sank those terrible teeth into Stodge's flesh. Then it fell back.

The werewolf was dead.

PC Squires was clambering to his feet. Stipo rushed up and grabbed Stodge's arm. Blood seeped from the four deep wounds, two on either side of his white fleshy arm. Stodge gazed at them as the blood trickled down his arm and dripped on to the floor.

'Is it dead?' asked the cop.

'Yes,' I said. 'Stodge shot it. With the last silver bullet. It worked.'

Then PC Squires noticed Stodge's arm, but he was so confused he didn't realize immediately what it meant.

'Did it bite you, lad?' he said, in a kindly voice.

Stodge didn't reply. His eyes were fixed on the running blood.

'Never mind,' Andy Squires went on, 'we'd best get you down to the hospital and get that seen to.'

Stipo was the only one who could explain. 'It's a werewolf bite,' he stuttered. 'Doctors can do . . . nothing.'

The policeman rocked back on his heels. He hesitated, then asked, 'Does that mean . . .'

We all looked at Stodge. He was staring at the four wounds and the blood coursing down his arm. He met our eyes. 'Yes,' he said, not needing to say more.

He'd been bitten by the werewolf. Now he would soon turn into one himself. Count Lupus was dead, but he'd left behind another werewolf to replace him.

'We can't just do nothing,' I said, almost screaming at them.

'So what do we do?' asked the policeman, his face contorted with grief.

'My people,' said Stipo. 'Take him to my people. There is an old woman who was once saved from a wolf bite. Perhaps she can help. But we'll have to be quick. Very quick.'

Stodge was still staring.

I'll never forget that desperate drive through the night. Police outriders on motorbikes with lights flashing and sirens blazing went ahead, and PC Squires' big hands were clenched on the steering wheel as he raced through the country lanes.

Slumped between me and Stipo in the back, Stodge never moved. His podgy face was white and unmoving. With his head down on his chest, I could see his rows of plump chins and his stomach bulging over his trousers. He was worth a hundred of those who used to tease him for being fat.

I held his hand. Ice.

Stipo turned over Stodge's other hand. Even in the dark of the car, I could see a few long hairs had appeared on his palm. 'Is where it starts,' said Stipo. 'On the hands, then everywhere.'

I felt the tears coming then and tried to wipe them away. Stipo and I sat there, each holding one of his hands. I was saying a quiet prayer. Stipo's face, as always, was a tearless mask. He had seen too much horror.

'Are we getting near?' I asked Chris, who was in the passenger seat.

'Another ten minutes,' he said. We couldn't

go any faster. The cop was driving like the wind, swerving round corners, rocketing along the straights.

'I think we are already too late,' Stipo muttered.

Then the vet and the policeman had a muffled conversation they obviously didn't want us to hear, but I caught the last sentence. 'In that case,' said Chris Maultby, 'we'll have to find another silver bullet.'

It took me a minute to realize what they meant. If Stodge did turn into a werewolf, they would shoot him. I couldn't bear the thought of that, however right it was.

Those last few miles seemed to take for ever. Eventually, we reached the town, passed the estates where people would be watching television, and finally bumped up to the waste ground in front of the old miners' cottages.

As always, the great bonfire was burning in the middle, casting shadows over the ground and the houses. Two or three people were gathered around the fire; others came out of the houses as we poured out of the car. They seemed to know what had happened.

Chris and the policeman carried the unconscious body of my friend through an open door and laid him on the floor. In the corner, huddled in a chair like a tiny broken bird, was an old woman. Between the headscarf and the layers of clothes, her face bore a mass of deep, furrowed lines and two small beady black eyes. In them was the wisdom of centuries of suffering.

Stipo gestured towards her. 'Laszla knows about such things. She is our last hope.'

Chapter 20

The old woman leaned forward to inspect Stodge and said something to Stipo. He held up a lantern and turned Stodge's hands so they were palm up. The hair was now becoming a thick coat which ran up over his wrists.

She spoke again in her own tongue. This time Stipo tilted up Stodge's face. Two sharp white fangs stuck out over his bottom lip. She said something else and Stipo turned to all of us. 'We only have seconds.'

Chris Maultby grabbed Stipo by the shoulder. 'But what can we do?'

Stipo seemed so sure of himself. 'She has seen it before. Once she was saved too.'

I couldn't stop myself. 'How are we gonna do it, Stipo?'

The room had filled up with gypsies. Their

strange foreign faces were full of the horror of what we were witnessing and they muttered among themselves. Stipo gave what sounded like instructions and two of the shawl-wrapped women left the room.

'Laszla says we must have the blood of a new-born child,' he said. 'That is all that can save him. Purity and innocence can destroy the evil of the werewolf's blood.'

'Where are we going to find a baby?' PC Squires asked.

Stipo had the answer. 'We have one here. Only two weeks old. But whether the mother will allow . . .' He left the sentence unfinished.

We stood there in silence around the motionless form of Stodge. As I watched and waited, it seemed that the vile hair on his hands grew longer, and the fangs seemed to stick out more and more.

Chris Maultby had been out to the car and had come back with his vet's medical kit. The gypsies crowded round as he opened it and produced a hypodermic needle. 'Sounds like we might need this,' he whispered to me.

The two older women in shawls came back into the room, leading a pretty young woman with huge dark eyes – and a baby in her arms. She looked worried and doubtful. She stared down at Stodge and flinched when she saw the clear signs of the werewolf.

Stipo instantly stepped forward and spoke and even though I couldn't understand the words I knew what he was saying. He was asking her for some of the baby's blood. Andy Squires, Chris Maultby and I all watched this drama, with the lantern light flickering around the room.

She listened, then hitched her baby up closer to her face, and shook her head. The word she said sounded like a cough. It meant one thing. No.

'She says she will not risk her baby's life,' Stipo interpreted. He was shaking his head in despair.

'But look,' I said, in panic, 'can't she see he's getting worse?'

The room was quiet now. Out of the quietness, out of the corner where she was huddled, came the voice of the old woman, Laszla. It was a creaky whine of a voice. Her unblinking eyes were fixed on the young mother.

'What's she saying?' I whispered to Stipo.

'Oh, that if another young mother many years ago in our old country had refused to give her baby's blood, then she – Laszla – would not be here today.'

The young mother shook her head again and made the No sound.

Laszla spoke again. Now she leaned forward, her huge eyes blazing with passion. Stipo whispered, 'Now she says that our people know the wickedness of the werewolves. Already they have taken three children. Does she want her child to be taken by them? This is the only way we can fight.'

All our eyes turned to the young mother. She jiggled her baby and touched its cheek with her finger. I looked around the room. In the yellow half-light, their faces looked as though they'd been carved in old, strong wood.

She said another word. Whatever it was it meant Yes.

Quick as a flash, Chris Maultby produced his instrument bag. He put one hand on the mother's shoulder and reassured her – if the words meant nothing to her, the kindly tone of his voice sure did. She laid the baby on Laszla's knee and Chris rubbed something on the baby's arm and gave a little wince himself as the needle moved softly under the skin.

Laszla spoke. 'Two drops,' said Stipo, acting as interpreter.

The baby gave a little cry, opened its eyes, then closed them again and continued sleeping.

With the needle in his hand, Chris knelt down beside Stodge. To me it looked far too late. His plump pink cheeks were covered in long dark hairs. His eyebrows were thickening and his hairline seemed to be coming down to meet them.

Worse were his fangs. They came nearly an inch over his chin. When the vet touched him he made a noise that sounded like a growl. Several of the people in the room flinched.

Chris rolled up Stodge's sleeve and quickly inserted the needle. I could only just see the tiny droplets of red blood. One push and they were gone.

I couldn't help it. 'Thank you, thank you!' I said to the young mother and I gave her and the baby a big kiss. She gave a slow nod of her head. She knew she'd done the right thing. As she left, there was a warm murmur.

Laszla rocked back in her seat and spoke again. 'Now we pray,' said Stipo.

Chapter 21

Everyone had gone now except the old woman. She kept her unblinking eyes on our friend as she passed rosary beads through her fingers and crooned a strange mumbling song.

Someone had laid a rough blue blanket over Stodge, but I could still see the way his face and arms were hideously marred by the teeth and coat of hair. He didn't look like my lovely Stodge any more.

I'd meant to watch over Stodge but the shock, the strain and the song that sounded like a lullaby were too much for me. My eyelids closed.

Suddenly I was awake again. Grey light showed at the windows. The old lady was asleep in her chair in the corner and Stipo was curled up on the floor next to Stodge.

I dropped to my knees and leaned over to look at him. It was our old Stodge back again! Fangs, hair – all gone! His funny podgy face was kinda peaceful and his little sausage fingers plucked at the blanket.

We'd saved Stodge!

Within seconds I had everyone awake. The room filled up with the gypsies, their solemn faces now wreathed in smiles, all talking, shaking hands, slapping backs, marvelling at the miracle.

Stipo ushered us all outside. 'Old lady, she say let him sleep,' he said, acting as interpreter again.

That was some breakfast, I can tell you. We ate at a long trestle table outside, and those gypsy mommas kept coming with the food. We had pancake-type things and delicious strong black bread and slices of salami-type stuff, all washed down with mugs of thick black coffee.

Me and Stipo, we stuffed the food into our mouths and couldn't stop grinning at each other. All the others kept shouting to Stipo and giving me the thumbs-up. That was some happy breakfast.

We kept going back in to look at Stodge, but we didn't disturb him because Laszla, the old girl, put her finger to her lips to tell us not to. He had turned on his side and was sleeping heavily. What made me and Stipo laugh was the way he'd got his thumb in his mouth. 'Too much baby blood,' I said.

We were having some more coffee outside when we looked up to see Stodge standing in the doorway, blinking sleepily. Everyone cheered. Wobbling a bit as he walked, he came over and sat with us.

He sat looking at the upturned palms of his hands. 'There was hair growing on them, wasn't there?' he asked me.

'Don't worry, Stodge,' I said, 'it's all over now. You're fine.'

He seemed to want to talk about it. 'It was like a dream. All the time I could hear that man's voice – that Count, like – and he was welcoming me to the Brotherhood of the Wolves.'

It was strange and frightening hearing him talk like this. It reminded me how close we'd been to the heart of evil.

'Trouble is, Lyddie,' he said, when I didn't reply, 'I thought he was right. I can remember the hatred I felt for you and Stipo – that's awful, isn't it?'

I patted his hand. 'It wasn't you. It was someone else taking over your mind.'

Chapter 22

Embarrassing? Hell (sorry Mom), it was killing, but it was really great too.

There we were, all three of us, on the school platform with the headmaster, and all the teachers, and the school governors and someone who was a Lord Lieutenant (whatever that is), with messages from Buckingham Palace.

And best of all, my mom and dad and Auntie Pauline were in the front row (saw you cry Auntie, don't deny it!).

And all those speeches! Someone must've tipped off the Lord Lieutenant guy because he said some things he couldn't possibly have known. 'I understand you three were known as The Outcasts,' he said, and Stipo nipped my butt (sorry, bum) when he said it. 'Well, you three have shown us what courage can do, and perhaps you have also taught us that kindness must not be forgotten too.'

Well, those cheers, I tell you. They rang and rang around our ears as they pinned these medal things on us, and I looked at Stipo, and you'd never guess. For the first time, after all the things we'd been through, there were tears running down his cheeks. I coulda kissed him but I thought that wouldn't help now he'd just got his street-cred to an all-time high.

Then afterwards, the best news of all. Dad said he'd got his business problems sorted out in court, and he'd won his business back.

'So if you want, Lydia,' he said, a bit kinda cautious, 'you can go back to your old school.'

'What?' I said, in real Geordie. 'And leave all my mates, like?'

'In that case,' he said, to my mother, 'it looks like we're moving north.'

THIS VOUCHER ENTITLES YOU TO 2 FOR 1 ENTRY TO:

Ride the nightmare! Take a boat trip on 'Judgement Day – Sentenced to Death'. It's a one-way journey to meet your maker in this terrifying recreation of 18th Century 'justice'.

Catch the plague at the York Dungeon! Take a spine-tingling tour around the plague-ravaged streets of 14th Century York in the company of your grisly guides.

The London Dungeon, Tooley Street, near London Bridge tube station. Telephone: 0171 403 7221 for further information and opening times.

The York Dungeon, 12 Clifford Street, York. Telephone: 01904 632599 for further information and opening times.

Terms and Conditions
1. This voucher will admit one adult or one child free to the London or York Dungeon when accompanied by an adult paying the single day adult admission.
2. This offer is not valid in conjunction with any other offer, promotion or voucher.
3. A child is classified as aged 4–14 years inclusive. Under 4's are admitted for free.
4. There is no cash alternative to this offer.
5. Photocopies of the voucher will not be accepted.
6. This offer is valid until 31 December 2000.